Miss Muffet
and the Spider
the

This edition first published in 2006 by
Sea-to-Sea Publications
1980 Lookout Drive
North Mankato
Minnesota 56003

Printed in China

Library of Congress Cataloging-in-Publication Data:

Graves, Sue.
  Miss Muffet and the spider / by Sue Graves.
     p. cm. — (Reading corner)
  Summary: A retelling of the nursery rhyme, in which the spider is surprised by a Miss
Muffet with attitude.
  ISBN 1-932889-99-X
  1. Nursery rhymes. 2. Children's poetry. [1. Spiders—Fiction. 2. Nursery rhymes.] I.
Title. II. Series.

PZ8.3.G7426Mi2005
[E]—dc22

                                                                              2004063626

9 8 7 6 5 4 3 2

Published by arrangement with the Watts Publishing Group Ltd, London

Series Editor: Jackie Hamley
Series Advisors: Linda Gambrell, Dr. Barrie Wade, Dr. Hilary Minns
Design: Peter Scoulding

Miss Muffet
and the Spider
the

Retold by
Sue Graves

Illustrated by
Sarah Warburton

SEA-TO-SEA
Mankato Collingwood London

Sue Graves
"I have four children and two cats so my house is very noisy! I teach children and love writing books. I hope you enjoy this one!"

Sarah Warburton
"I love drawing and fairy tales, but I'm very, very afraid of spiders!"

Little Miss Muffet

sat on a tuffet,

eating her curds
and whey.

9

Down came...

11

...a spider,

13

who sat down
beside her,

15

and tried,

17

and tried,

19

to frighten Miss Muffet
away!

23

Notes for parents and teachers

READING CORNER has been structured to provide maximum support for new readers. The stories may be used by adults for sharing with young children. Primarily, however, the stories are designed for newly independent readers, whether they are reading these books in bed at night, or in the reading corner at school or in the library.

Starting to read alone can be a daunting prospect. READING CORNER helps by providing visual support and repeating words and phrases, while making reading enjoyable. These books will develop confidence in the new reader, and encourage a love of reading that will last a lifetime!

If you are reading this book with a child, here are a few tips:

1. Make reading fun! Choose a time to read when you and the child are relaxed and have time to share the story.

2. Encourage children to reread the story, and to retell the story in their own words, using the illustrations to remind them what has happened.

3. Give praise! Remember that small mistakes need not always be corrected.

READING CORNER covers three grades of early reading ability, with three levels at each grade. Each level has a certain number of words per story, indicated by the number of bars on the spine of the book, to allow you to choose the right book for a young reader:

GRADE 1	GRADE 2	GRADE 3
50 words	130 words	250 words
70 words	160 words	350 words
100 words	200 words	450 words